the park

the park

by RICHARD LEWIS

photographs by HELEN BUTTFIELD

SIMON & SCHUSTER • NEW YORK

First Printing

Library of Congress Catalog Card Number: 68-28917
Manufactured in the United States of America
Printed by Sanders Printing Corp., New York
Bound by Economy Book Binding Corp., New Jersey

To Danny

On any day there is a path

from city streets

and city walls,

a path to the park.

Even on a winter's day

the silver face of ice,

frosted arms,

and waiting silence,

waiting

for a bird's song.

In one morning's sunrise

spring comes.

In one day's delight

a thousand whispers....

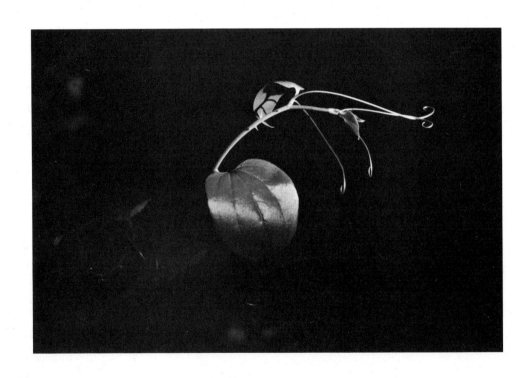

Secrets told to still water,

heard by a summer sky,

echo in caverns everywhere.

Who made the day run short again?

What rainbow shed its colors in the morning air?

Where is the feast

of autumn?

From city walls,

city streets,

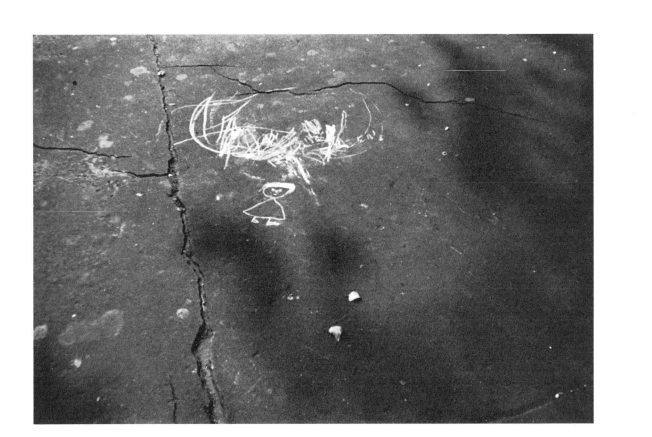

on any day,

there is a path.